Liza

Best Friends Series
Book 3

David M. Sargent, Jr. and his friends all live in a small town in northwest Arkansas. While he lies in the hammock, the dogs (left to right: Spike, Emma, Daphne and Mary) play ball, dig holes or bark at kitty cats. When not playing in the yard, they travel around the United States, meeting children and writing stories.

Liza

Best Friends Series
Book 3

David M. Sargent, Jr.

Illustrated by Debbie Farmer

Ozark Publishing, Inc.
P.O. Box 228
Prairie Grove, AR 72753

Cataloging-in-Publication Data

Sargent, David M., 1966–
    Liza / by David M. Sargent, Jr. ;
illustrated by Debbie Farmer.—Prairie Grove, AR;
Ozark Publishing, c2007.
    p. cm. (Best friends series ; 3)

    "Good work"—Cover.
    SUMMARY: When Jake and his dad can't
find a missing cow who is due to calve, they
head back to the ranch. They have to mend a
fence. Liza the Border Collie does not give up
the search. Will she find the cow in time?

    ISBN 1-59381-062-8 (hc)
            1-59381-063-6 (pbk)

    1. Dogs—Juvenile fiction.
[1. Dogs—Fiction. 2. Border Collie—Fiction.]
I. Farmer, Debbie, 1958– ill. II. Title.
III. Series.

    PZ8.3.S2355Li 2007
    [E]—dc21   2003099199

Inspired by

a Border Collie we had on the farm.

Dedicated to

all boys and girls who love to watch dogs work cattle and horses.

Foreword

When Jake and his dad can't find a missing cow that is due to calve, they head back to the ranch. They have to mend a fence. Liza the Border Collie does not give up the search. Will she find the cow in time?

Contents

If you would like to have the author of the Best Friends Series visit your school free of charge, please call 1-800-321-5671.

One

The Border Collie

Liza the Border Collie was on the floor beside the bed of her master. The teenage boy was sound asleep. Suddenly the bedroom door opened, and a tall man entered the room.

"Time to get up, Jake," his father said. "We have a lot of work to do today."

The boy sat up and yawned. "Okay, Dad," he said. "Liza and I will be ready in a minute."

As the man shut the door, Liza stood up and licked the boy's hand. Jake smiled and jumped out of bed. Soon the boy and the dog hurried down the stairs.

After Jake finished breakfast, he walked outside. His dad was waiting on the porch.

"Son," he said, "I think one of our cows is missing. She's due to have a calf this week. Yesterday she was not with the rest of the herd."

Liza watched as Jake and his father saddled their horses. A short time later, they rode their horses toward the big pasture. Liza then followed a safe distance behind.

Two

A Cow Is Missing

They searched the valleys, the hills and the pasture. Liza followed as they rode through the cattle.

They scouted among the trees and thickets. But they did not find the missing cow. Finally, Jake's father reined his horse to a halt.

"We'd better give up for now, Jake," he said. "We have to mend that broken fence before dark."

Jake said, "Maybe we can look for her after we get through with the fence. I hope she'll be okay until then."

Liza stopped and sat down as the two riders turned back toward the ranch. The two-year-old black and white Border Collie whined softly.

A moment later, Liza sniffed the air, then raced toward a ravine. A cow was upside down in the narrow groove.

The Border Collie barked twice. Then she turned and ran as hard as she could toward the ranch.

Jake and his dad had reached the ranch and were unsaddling their horses, when Liza ran into the barn.

Three

The Upside-down Cow

Liza barked at Jake. Then she ran back to the barn door.

"What's the matter with Liza?" Jake's dad asked.

"I don't know," Jake replied.

They watched as Liza barked again and ran toward the barn door.

"She wants us to follow her," Jake said.

"We need to mend fence," his father growled.

Liza barked again and ran from the barn.

"Okay," his father said. "But she better have a good reason for this."

Soon Liza was running across the pasture toward the ravine. Two horses and riders followed close behind. As Liza ran down the hill toward the missing cow, she again barked.

"That dog of yours has found that cow!" Jake's dad exclaimed.

"Look, Dad!" Jake yelled. "The cow has had her calf. I see it!"

Jake and his father quickly roped the cow. They stood her on her feet, and soon the little baby was switching his tail as he ate his first meal.

Jake hugged the dog. "Liza, you saved that mama and her baby," he said.

"She's a good Border Collie, Son," Jake's dad said. "You're doing a good job training her."

"We gave up trying to find her, but you didn't, did you? You are a good dog. You're my best friend!"